The Great Big Elephant and the Very Small Elephant

BARBARA SEULING

SCHOLASTIC BOOK SERVICES
NEW YORK · TORONTO · LONDON · AUCKLAND · SYDNEY · TOKYO

Copyright © 1977 by Barbara Seuling. All rights reserved. This edition is published by Scholastic Book Services, a division of Scholastic Magazines, Inc., 50 West 44th Street, New York, N.Y. 10036, by arrangement with Crown Publishers, Inc.

12 11 10 9 8 7 6 5 4 3 2 1   2   9/7 0 1 2 3 4/8

Printed in the U.S.A.   07

FOR WINNETTE

The Great Big Elephant Goes to Work in the Circus

One day a letter came for the Great Big Elephant from his cousin in Paris.

"I have the mumps," it said. "Can you come and take my place in the Circus Maximus until I am better?"

The Great Big Elephant ran right over to the Very Small Elephant's house to tell his best friend the news.

"Will you go?" asked the Very Small Elephant.

"Of course," said the Great Big Elephant. "I must go. Someone needs me."

"But I need you," said the Very Small Elephant.

"Oh, that's very nice of you to say," said the Great Big Elephant. "But my cousin *really* needs me. He's sick." And, after reading the letter over once more, he went home to pack.

In a little while, the Very Small Elephant arrived at the Great Big Elephant's house with a huge bandage on his head.

"What happened?" cried the Great Big Elephant.

"I'm sick," said the Very Small Elephant. "I need you. I have a headache."

"A headache?" said the Great Big Elephant. "You don't bandage your head when you have a headache."

The Very Small Elephant took off his bandage and sadly walked away.

A little later, the Very Small Elephant was back at the Great Big
Elephant's house. This time he had a bandage tied around his trunk.

"What happened now?" asked the Great Big Elephant.

"I'm sick," said the Very Small Elephant. "I need you. I have a cold
in my nose."

"You don't wear a bandage for a cold," said the Great Big Elephant.
"I think you are playing games."

He took the bandage off the Very Small Elephant's trunk, gave him
a pat on the behind, and sent him home.

A short time afterward, the Very Small Elephant was back again. A huge bandage was wrapped all around his stomach.

"Now what?" asked the Great Big Elephant.

"I'm sick. I need you. I have a bellyache," said the Very Small Elephant.

"You don't wear a bandage when you have a bellyache," said the Great Big Elephant. "You are trying to fool me again. Now let me get ready."

"I don't want you to go," said the Very Small Elephant. "If you go, I will be all alone, and I don't like being alone. I am afraid."

The Great Big Elephant stopped packing and went over to the Very Small Elephant.

"I don't want to leave you, but I must," said the Great Big Elephant. "And I know that you can take care of yourself while I am gone. It will only be for a little while."

A tear fell down the Very Small Elephant's trunk.

"How little?" he said.

"Just until the mumps go away," said the Great Big Elephant. "Then I will come back."

"Okay," said the Very Small Elephant. "But I won't like it one bit."

When the Great Big Elephant was ready to leave, they were both very sad.

"Don't forget to write," said the Very Small Elephant.

"I won't," said the Great Big Elephant. "And don't forget to water my plants."

"I won't," said the Very Small Elephant.

It was not easy to say good-bye, but they did.

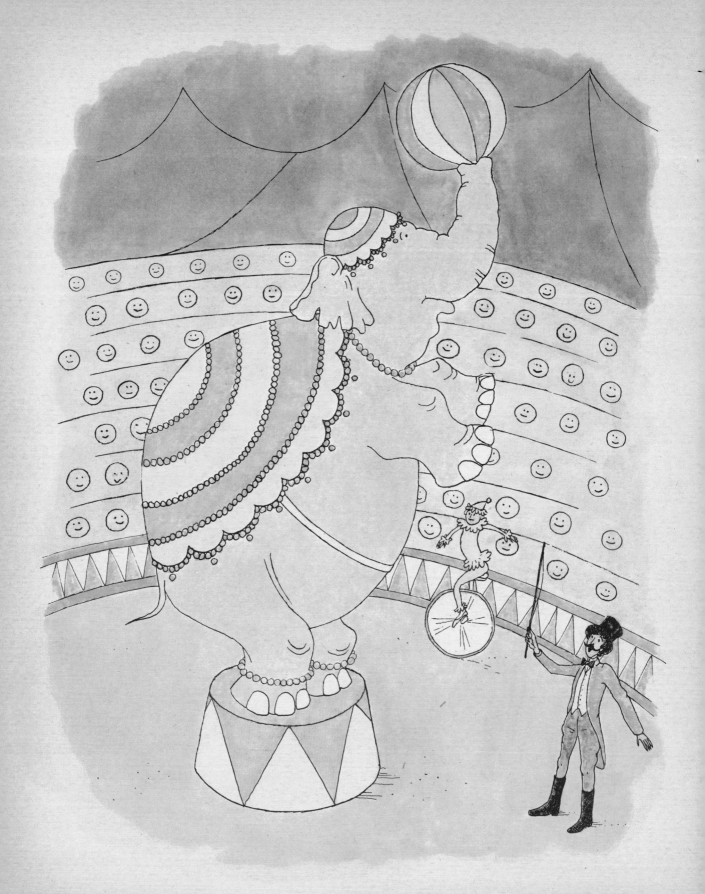

Five days later, a letter came from the Great Big Elephant. It said that being in the Circus Maximus was very exciting, and that he got to wear beautiful costumes with thousands of beads on them. It also said:

My cousin's mumps are better and I will be home in three days.

Love,

The Great Big Elephant

The Very Small Elephant put the stamp from his letter into his stamp collection, watered all the plants, and before you know it, the Great Big Elephant was home.

He brought some beads for the Very Small Elephant, who wore them everywhere, even to bed.

And for many days to come, the Great Big Elephant told the Very Small Elephant of his days with the Circus Maximus.

Great-Aunt Matilda Comes to Visit

Early one morning a telegram arrived for the Very Small Elephant.
It said:

COMING TO VISIT FOR THREE DAYS STOP

ARRIVING TOMORROW AFTERNOON STOP

LOVE GREAT AUNT MATILDA

"Oh dear, oh dear," said the Very Small Elephant.

He ran right over to the Great Big Elephant's house and showed him the telegram.

"What shall I do?" cried the Very Small Elephant.

"It's very easy," said the Great Big Elephant. "First you will have to tidy up your house. Great-Aunts are very fussy about housekeeping. Then you will have to decide where Great-Aunt Matilda will sleep so that she will be comfortable. And then," said the Great Big Elephant, "you will have to cook wonderful meals for her and take her to interesting places."

"Oh dear, oh dear," cried the Very Small Elephant. "Maybe I should just telegraph her back and say she can't come, that I've gone to sea, or have died of the rot."

"No, no," said the Great Big Elephant. "You can't do that to Great-Aunts. They always know."

"But I am a terrible housekeeper," said the Very Small Elephant. "I can't cook. I have only one bed—mine. And I am not very good at thinking up things to do, especially with old ladies. What am I going to do?"

"Don't worry," said the Great Big Elephant. "I will help you."

That afternoon the Great Big Elephant arrived at the Very Small Elephant's house with a folding cot under one arm and a feather duster under the other.

"You will have to sleep on this," he said, opening the cot. "Great-Aunt Matilda will sleep in your bed."

"I am not going to like this at all," muttered the Very Small Elephant.

The Great Big Elephant began tidying up. He dusted everywhere—
even under the bed. He washed and ironed the curtains, straightened
the pictures on the wall, cleaned the fingerprints off the jelly jar, and
polished the doorknob until he could see himself in it.

The Very Small Elephant hardly noticed. All he could think about
was the next three days and how he would survive them.

The next day, when Great-Aunt Matilda arrived, the Great Big
Elephant sat her down in a comfortable chair, handed her a grape
tonic, and listened to stories about her arthritis and her trip.

The Very Small Elephant sat close by, worrying. "How will I ever
do it?" he wondered.

Later, Great-Aunt Matilda took a nap. While she was napping, the Great Big Elephant pulled vegetables out of the garden, he washed and peeled them, and made a huge pot of stew with dumplings. Then he pounded and beat a pile of dough, shaped it into loaves, and baked some bread. Finally, he made a coconut pie.

The Very Small Elephant sat at the kitchen table, wondering how to make it through two more days.

After dinner, they talked some more and played checkers until they got sleepy. Then the Great Big Elephant went back to his house and slept in his bed. Great-Aunt Matilda slept happily in the Very Small Elephant's bed.

The Very Small Elephant tossed and turned all night on the little cot.

In the morning, the Great Big Elephant arrived, looking bright and cheerful. The Very Small Elephant looked terrible.

After a splendid breakfast, they took Great-Aunt Matilda shopping. She bought a hat with flowers on it and a lacy handkerchief with her initials in the corner. For all her nieces and nephews, she bought peanut fudge.

In the afternoon, they went to a concert and ate pineapple ice cream sundaes afterward. In the evening, they went down to the waterhole for a swim.

The Very Small Elephant felt a little better, but still he worried. "There is still one whole day to go," he thought.

The following day, they packed a basket and had a picnic with lots of peanuts and bananas and marshmallows, right next to a waterfall.

"I am having a wonderful time," announced Great-Aunt Matilda.
She reached into her bag and took out her camera. "I hate to leave.
But before I go, let's take some pictures." They took plenty of
snapshots of everybody for Great-Aunt Matilda's family album.

Later that day, the Great Big Elephant and the Very Small Elephant took Great-Aunt Matilda to the airport. They said good-bye to her and wished her a safe trip home.

"Great-Aunt Matilda isn't so bad," said the Very Small Elephant. The Great Big Elephant smiled.

"I really liked having her here," said the Very Small Elephant. The Great Big Elephant nodded.

"And it was easy!" said the Very Small Elephant. The Great Big Elephant sighed.

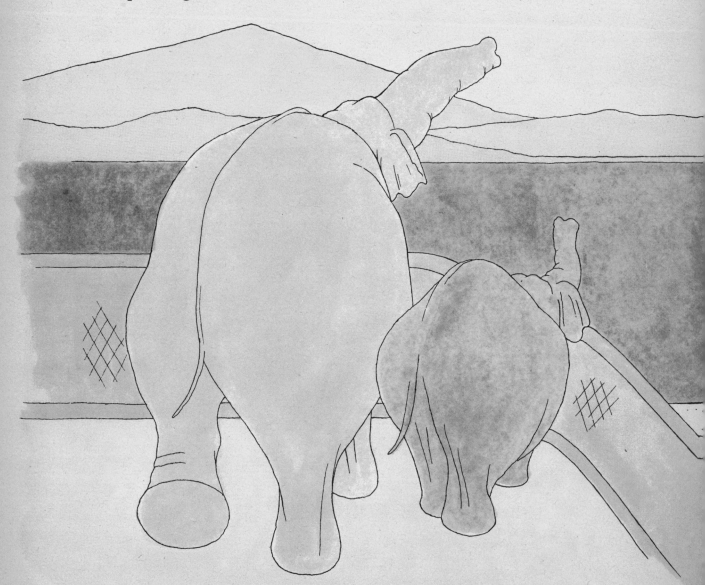

"Maybe I'll invite her to come again," said the Very Small Elephant.
"Fine," said the Great Big Elephant, "but not *too* soon!"
The Very Small Elephant laughed.
And they both went home and took a long, long nap.

The Great Big Elephant
and the Very Small Elephant Play Games

The Great Big Elephant and the Very Small Elephant were playing, when they came to a pond.

"Let's run through it," said the Very Small Elephant. He splashed across, making a great mess, and came out on the other side.

"Okay," said the Great Big Elephant, and he stepped in. But he was so heavy that he sank into the mud bottom and got stuck.

The Great Big Elephant felt foolish. But the Very Small Elephant pulled him out and cleaned him up.

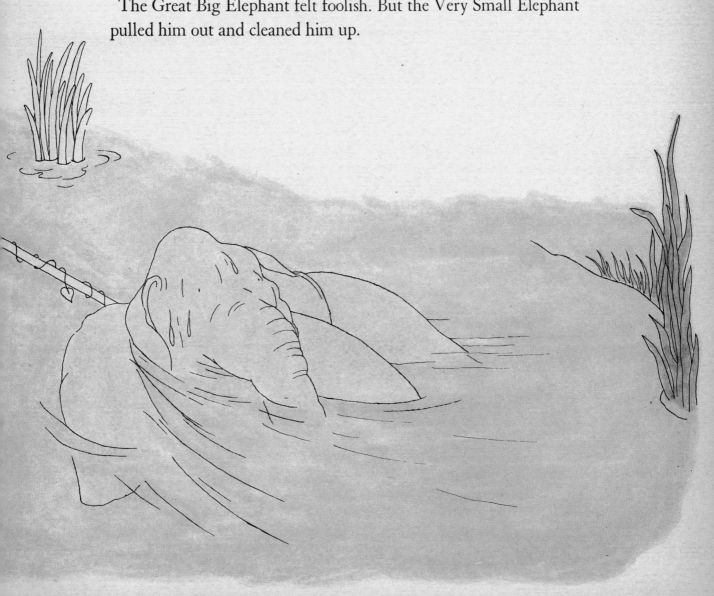

Then they played hide-and-seek. The Great Big Elephant couldn't find the Very Small Elephant for a very long time because the Very Small Elephant hid behind the banana trees so well. When the Great Big Elephant hid, the Very Small Elephant found him right away because he stuck out in so many places.

"You're it," he heard, over and over again.

Next they played tag. The Great Big Elephant was always caught, because he couldn't run very fast, but the Very Small Elephant kept getting away.

The Great Big Elephant was unhappy. "I don't want to play anymore," he said.

"Why?" said the Very Small Elephant.

"I am not as good at things as you are," said the Great Big Elephant. "You can splash better than I can, hide better than I can, run better than I can. You can do everything better. I am no good at all."

"That's not true," said the Very Small Elephant. "You are good at things too."

"No, I'm not," said the Great Big Elephant. "You're just saying that." He started to walk away. The Very Small Elephant followed him, trying to cheer him up.

"You make friends better," said the Very Small Elephant. "If it weren't for you, I would not have any friends at all."

"Monkey and Parrot are your friends," said the Great Big Elephant. "And so are Ostrich and Hippo and Lion."

"Yes," said the Very Small Elephant, "but you were the one who made friends with them. You invited them over for tea and gingerbread."

The Great Big Elephant thought about it. "Maybe I did make friends first. But that doesn't mean anything," he said. "What matters is that we are all friends *now*."

"Remember when you got us the juicy leaves from the top of the bam-bam tree?" said the Very Small Elephant.

"Oh, that was nothing," said the Great Big Elephant. "Anyone could have helped you get those leaves."

"But anyone didn't do it. *You* did," cried the Very Small Elephant. "And it was you who thought of it."

"You're my friend and you're only trying to make me feel better," said the Great Big Elephant.

"Well, what about when Great-Aunt Matilda came to visit and I didn't know what to do? You came right over and helped. If it weren't for you," said the Very Small Elephant, "I don't know what I would have done."

"I guess I did help a little," said the Great Big Elephant.
He stopped short. The Very Small Elephant stopped too. There in
the middle of the path stood Rinaldo. Rinaldo loved to fight.
"If you try to pass here," he shouted, *"you'll be sorry!"*

The Great Big Elephant was angry. He looked to see that the Very Small Elephant was behind him. Then he pulled himself up as big and as tall as he could, and snorted: "YOU OUGHT TO BE ASHAMED OF YOURSELF. GET OUT OF MY WAY OR I'LL PUT A KNOT IN YOUR TAIL!"

No one had ever dared to speak to Rinaldo that way before. His knees shook and his teeth rattled. He backed away until he was well into the jungle. Then he turned and ran as fast as he could.

The Very Small Elephant came out from behind his large friend. "You were wonderful," he said. "I couldn't have done that. Rinaldo would have flattened me!"

The Great Big Elephant blushed. "Let's play," he said. And even though he didn't win too many games, they had a lot of fun.